EVERYBODY'S HOME

A Lola Jones BOOK

JONATHAN EIG

illustrated by
ALICIA TEBA GODOY

ALBERT WHITMAN & CO.
Chicago, Illinois

For Heidi—JE

To my friends and family, always—ATG

Library of Congress Cataloging-in-Publication data
is on file with the publisher.

Text copyright © 2021 by Jonathan Eig
Illustrations copyright © 2021 by Albert Whitman & Company
Illustrations by Alicia Teba Godoy
Hardcover edition first published in the United States of America
in 2021 by Albert Whitman & Company
Paperback edition first published in the United States of America
in 2021 by Albert Whitman & Company
ISBN 978-0-8075-6574-2 (hardcover)
ISBN 978-0-8075-6576-6 (paperback)
ISBN 978-0-8075-6575-9 (ebook)

Printed in the United States of America
10 9 8 7 6 5 4 3 2 1 LB 26 25 24 23 22 21

Design by Aphelandra

For more information about Albert Whitman & Company,
visit our website at www.albertwhitman.com.

TABLE OF CONTENTS

1. Hey, Ho! Nobody Home! 1

2. Stop! Stop! Stop! 5

3. Annoying Parrot 13

4. Dinner and Dance Party 18

5. School Newspaper Article 23

6. Weather Charts 27

7. Mocha Sings 36

8. Fire Drill 40

9. Stomp and Sing 50

10. Snow Day 54

11. Sledding 63

12. Snowman 70

13. Another Article, Another Song 74

14. Winter Concert Review 80

15. Everybody's Home 84

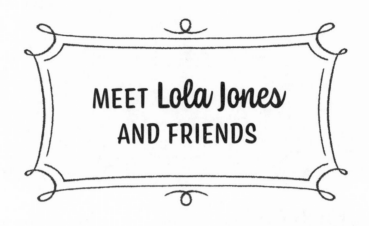

MEET Lola Jones AND FRIENDS

Hi! I'm Lola.

I love books and I love adventure. When I'm trying to solve a problem, I know I can count on my family, my friends, and characters from my favorite books!

Lola Jones

Lillian Jones
I'm Lola's mother. I love playing soccer and having crazy dance parties with my daughter.

Grampa Ed
I'm Lola's grandfather. That kid cracks me up. I try to pretend I'm grumpy sometimes, but she never falls for it.

Mrs. Gunderson
I'm Lola's teacher, and I love my third graders. My favorite book is *Charlotte's Web* by E.B. White.

Maya and Fayth
We're Lola's best friends. Whatever wild plan she's hatching, we're always there to help out!

1.
Hey, Ho! Nobody Home!

Lola Jones stood in the first row of the chorus in music class. She fidgeted, shifting from one leg to the other.

Ms. Nedick, the music teacher, stood at the podium in front of the children. She was tall and graceful, with round curls and pretty blue-framed glasses.

Ms. Nedick tapped her conductor's baton on her podium. *Tap-tap-tap!*

"Class, there are three weeks left until our Winter Concert," she said. "Let's try again..."

The students in Lola's class had been working

a long time to prepare for the Winter Concert. They were supposed to have memorized all the songs by now, but one song—"Hey, Ho! Nobody Home!"—still gave them trouble.

Ms. Nedick lifted her conductor's baton in the air.

"One and two and three and four and…"

The class began to sing in a wishy-washy way.

Music class was usually fun, Lola thought, but not lately. That song was ruining everything.

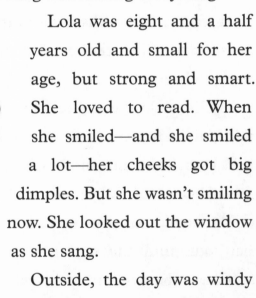

Lola was eight and a half years old and small for her age, but strong and smart. She loved to read. When she smiled—and she smiled a lot—her cheeks got big dimples. But she wasn't smiling now. She looked out the window as she sang.

Outside, the day was windy and gray. A bus stopped for passengers, its brakes squealing.

Lola imagined the squeal was really Chester, the little cricket from her new favorite book, *The Cricket in Times Square,* tuning up his wings to make music. She couldn't wait to get home and read the next chapter.

"Enthusiasm, class! Enthusiasm!" Ms. Nedick said, as her baton bounced up and down on the air. "This song is full of energy and joy!"

Energy? Joy? Lola's brows knitted. She didn't feel energy or joy from this song. A quick glance at the faces of her classmates in the rows behind her didn't convince her that they felt these things from the song, either. Her classmates slouched and fidgeted, like Lola.

But at the end of Lola's row, her friend Maya stood up straight, and her voice rang out loud and strong. Maya was always a model student and loved to sing— and seemed to have no trouble at all with the lyrics of "Hey, Ho! Nobody Home!"

"Good, Maya, very nice!" Ms. Nedick nodded and smiled at Maya.

"Louder please, Lola!" Ms. Nedick said.

Oh, how Lola wished she were home, reading *The Cricket in Times Square!*

2.
Stop! Stop! Stop!

A week later, the class still hadn't figured out "Hey, Ho! Nobody Home!" Maya was still the only one singing clearly and getting the words right.

"No! No!" Ms. Nedick was saying. "Focus on the lyrics, please, everyone! Begin again!"

"Hey, ho. Nobody home..." the class sang.

The first line of the song was easy. Lola and her classmates got that much right. But the rest was a big muddle.

"Meat for fish, no money for your lungs!" Lola sang.

"Meet my fish, no mummies having fun!" sang Fayth.

"Eat your fish, your tummy has the runs!" sang the new girl, Antoinette.

Peter Pincus barked out a laugh and sang: "Antoinette's tummy has the runs!" And then he hooted with more laughter. Lots of students in the class laughed too.

Antoinette's cheeks turned red.

"Stop! Stop! Stop!" Ms. Nedick shouted. She waved her hands in the air. "Peter, that's enough! Apologize to Antoinette for being rude—*and* for interrupting the class!"

Peter Pincus mumbled an apology.

Ms. Nedick took a deep breath. She did not look happy. "We have only two weeks until our Winter Concert," she reminded the class. "Doesn't *anyone* remember the words to this song?"

No hands went up. Not even Maya's.

"We've practiced so many times," Ms. Nedick said. "And you're doing so well with the other songs... I don't see what's so difficult about this one!"

The class stood silently, watching Ms. Nedick.

Ms. Nedick watched the class.

At last she shook her head. "Never mind... Let's try again, a little slower this time." She

tapped her baton on the podium twice and then raised it in the air. "Heads up, shoulders back, eyes on me, everyone!"

The students stood up a bit straighter.

"One and two and...."

But, suddenly, Peter Pincus made a rude noise out of the side of his mouth.

Everybody giggled.

Ms. Nedick stepped from behind the podium and called Peter Pincus to the front of the room. "If you cannot respect the music, then you will not sing. Please stand here silently until you choose to respect the music. Do you understand?"

Now Peter Pincus was embarrassed. His head was down, but he nodded.

"Good." Ms. Nedick walked back behind the podium. Heat from the radiator made the room

stuffy and the children drowsy.

"Ready? Repeat after me, please!" Ms. Nedick raised her

baton in the air again and sang: "Hey, ho! Nobody home!"

The students sang loudly and strongly: "Hey, ho! Nobody home!"

Ms. Nedick smiled and nodded, and continued: "No meat, nor fish, nor money have I none!"

"No meat, no fish, no monkeys on the tongue!" sang Lola.

"No feet, no fish, no running in the sun!" sang Gianna, who was standing in the row behind Lola.

"No beets to squish, no bunnies in the dung!" sang Lorenzo.

"I want some cheese! Some cheesy, cheesy cheese!" sang Peter Pincus, loudest of all, prompting more giggles from the class.

"Stop! Stop! Stop!" Ms. Nedick shouted again. She

9

sat Peter Pincus facing away from the class. Then she stood with her lips pursed and her hands on her hips. The class quieted down and watched as Ms. Nedick walked around and around, cooling down from her aggravation. She finally stopped and took a breath.

Lola raised her hand.

"Yes, Lola?"

"Ms. Nedick, I *really* don't understand this song. Can you tell us what it's about?"

"Children," Ms. Nedick said, "can anyone tell Lola what this song is about?"

The room fell silent.

Ms. Nedick asked again: "Can *anyone* tell Lola what this song is about?"

The students shifted in their places, but everyone remained silent, including Maya.

"Ms. Nedick," Lola asked softly, "have you ever read a book called *The Cricket in Times Square*?"

Ms. Nedick shook her head no.

"It's about a cricket named Chester," Lola continued. "He makes beautiful music with his wings. He *loves* the music, and that's why it's so good."

"That's very interesting, Lola," Ms. Nedick said. "But what does it have to do with our rehearsal?"

"Well," Lola said, "don't you think we'd sound better if we picked a song that we loved? Can we choose another song?"

"Yeah, a song that we like!" said Fayth.

"A song that's fun!" said Tommy.

"A song about cheese!" said Peter Pincus.

"Quiet, please! Quiet!" Ms. Nedick tapped her baton on the podium sharply.

Everyone hushed.

"'Hey, Ho! Nobody Home!' is a beautiful, traditional holiday song!" Ms. Nedick said. "I sang this song in the school choir when I was your age. It's about people who are walking the streets singing Christmas carols and sharing food and drink. Even when they get to a house where no one's home to share their food and drink with, they're still happy."

"Oh, I get it," said Lola, though she still didn't like the song.

Ms. Nedick tapped the podium. "Let's try one more time."

Lola raised her hand, again.

But this time, Ms. Nedick didn't call on her. "Repeat after me," Ms. Nedick said to the class, and she began to sing, "Hey, ho! Nobody home..."

Lola moved her lips, but she didn't sing.

She was too busy thinking of how to change Ms. Nedick's mind.

3.

Annoying Parrot

After school, Grampa Ed walked Lola, Fayth, and Maya home.

Once she was in her apartment, Lola ate a snack of peanut butter on apple slices, with a glass of milk. Then she went to visit her grandfather. Grampa Ed lived in the same building as Lola and her mother. Grampa Ed lived on the first floor. Lola and her mother lived on the second floor.

"Knock-knock," Lola said as she opened the door to her grandfather's apartment.

"Who's there?" came the deep, scratchy voice of Grampa Ed.

"Annoying parrot," said Lola.

"Annoying parrot, who?" asked Grampa Ed.

"Annoying parrot, who?" asked Lola.

There was a long pause.

"Wait! Is that the whole joke?" Grampa Ed scratched his head.

"Yes, Grampa, that's the whole joke." Lola put her hands on her hips. "It's an *annoying parrot*, so it repeats whatever it hears. Get it?"

"Yeah, I get it. But I don't think it's funny. You're usually a funny kid. You can do better than that." Grampa Ed stood up from his kitchen table, where he was drinking coffee. Garbo, Grampa Ed's cute little black-and-white dog, skittered across the floor and ran in happy circles around Lola's legs.

Grampa Ed was a big man with big arms and a big belly. His head was shiny on top, with white hair on the sides. He had a white beard too. He had lots of tattoos, including one on his left arm that read, "Whatever Lola Wants." His apartment, which was also his art studio, smelled of coffee

and pencil eraser and oil paint and Grampa Ed.

"O.K.," Lola said. "I admit it wasn't my best joke. But that's because I have a lot on my mind."

"What's on your mind, kid? Worried that you're losing your sense of humor now that you're growing up?"

"No, it's a *serious* problem, Grampa!"

"That's what happens when people lose their sense of humor. They develop serious problems!"

"Grampa, would you *please* listen? Ms. Nedick is making us sing this horrible, terrible song for

15

the Winter Concert. I asked her nicely if she would let us pick a new song, but she said no. And I don't think she's being fair. Shouldn't we be allowed to pick at least one song on our own?"

"That seems reasonable," Grandpa Ed said. "What's the name of this horrible, terrible song you don't want to sing?"

"It's called 'Hey, Ho! Nobody Home!'"

Grampa Ed spat a little coffee out of his mouth as he laughed. "Are you kidding me? We sang that song when *I* was in school a zillion years ago! I still remember how it goes..." Grampa Ed began to sing in a big, booming voice: "Hey, ho! Nobody home..." He paused. "La, la, la, la, glubby, glubby, glub."

Garbo heard

the singing and started to howl.

"See, even Garbo doesn't like it!" Lola said.

"It's just a song, kid. Why get so upset?"

"But it's *not* just a song, Grampa. It's about us kids. We should be allowed to pick our own songs. In *The Cricket in Times Square*—that's my new favorite book, by the way—no one tells Chester Cricket what songs to play. He plays the songs he loves. He *chooses*. That's why his songs sound so good. What's the point of singing if you don't sing with feeling?"

"Well, what would Chester do if someone made him play a song he didn't like?"

"I don't know," Lola said, rubbing her chin in thought. "But I'm sure he'd think of something!"

4.
Dinner and
Dance Party

Lola's mother made a giant pan of lasagna for dinner that night. She set it in the center of the table.

"Oh, wow!" Lola said. "That smells so good!"

Lillian Jones smiled and brought some garlic bread to the table.

Grampa Ed, who often came upstairs to share meals with Lillian and Lola, walked into the kitchen, whistling a tune that Lola didn't recognize. He had made a salad. The salad had so many ingredients Lola wasn't sure she could identify them all. She spotted three kinds of

leafy greens, some red tomatoes, yellow tomatoes, onions, avocado, almonds, cucumbers, red
peppers, yellow peppers, green beans, croutons,
black olives, and garbanzo beans.

"I call this my Garbage-Can Salad," said
Grampa Ed.

"Yuck, Grampa! That's not a nice name!" said
Lola. "No one wants to eat from a garbage can!"

"Good! More for me!" Grampa Ed pulled the
salad bowl toward him.

"I'll eat it because it looks delicious," Lola said,
"but I'm going to call it the Picnic-Basket Salad.
Grampa, please pass me the Picnic-Basket Salad."

"Sorry, that's not on the menu, kid, but we
have a lovely Garbage-Can Salad. It's right here.
Would you like to try it?"

"Actually, Grampa, I'll just have some of this
lovely Picnic-Basket Salad...."

Lola grabbed the bowl and scooped salad
onto her plate while Grampa Ed took a piece of
lasagna. Garbo waited under the table in case any
scraps fell to the floor—and Grampa Ed always

made sure a few scraps fell to the floor.

"How was school today?" Lillian Jones asked.

"Mostly good," Lola said.

"Mostly?"

"Uh-oh," Grampa Ed said with a smile. "Here it comes!"

"Ms. Nedick, the music teacher, is making us sing a song no one likes, and I'm trying to persuade her to let the kids pick a better song.

But she won't listen to me. Don't you think kids should be able to pick their own songs?"

"Hey, ho, no, no, no, no!" Grampa Ed sang as he slid another helping of lasagna onto the spatula. Garbo barked. "If I had to sing 'Hey, Ho! Nobody Home!' you should have to sing it!" Grampa Ed laughed with his mouth full.

"Oh," said Lillian Jones. "I remember that song. I had to sing it too. It's traditional!"

"That's what Ms. Nedick said. But what does *traditional* mean?" Lola asked.

"It means handed down from a long time ago," Lola's mother said.

"Like Groundhog Day?" Lola asked. "We learned about that in school. That's when everybody waits for a groundhog to stick his head out of the ground. If the groundhog sees its shadow, winter will last six more weeks."

"Yes, that's an example of a tradition," Lola's mother said.

"But it's not real, is it? The groundhog can't really tell how long winter is going to last, right?

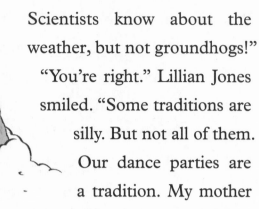

Scientists know about the weather, but not groundhogs!"

"You're right." Lillian Jones smiled. "Some traditions are silly. But not all of them. Our dance parties are a tradition. My mother used to dance with me, and her mother danced with her. And now I dance with you."

"But you and your mother probably danced to really old songs, like Beethoven! Now we dance to new songs! Fun songs!" Lola rubbed her chin. "That means traditions can change, right?"

"Well, yes, I guess it does!" said Lillian Jones.

"Grampa," Lola Jones said. "I thought of a good, new tradition. Let's have this yummy Picnic-Basket Salad every Monday night from now on."

"Hmm," Grampa Ed said. "That reminds me of a song: 'Hey, ho! Nobody home! Garbage-Can Salad is yummy-yum-yum!'"

5.
School Newspaper Article

After dinner, Lola and her mother sat in the living room reading books. Lola's cat, Mocha, curled up in her lap.

"Mom," Lola said, looking up from her book, "what's a newsstand?"

In Lola's book, Chester Cricket lived in a newsstand in a subway station in New York City. One night, he and his friends Harry Cat and Tucker Mouse had a party. Chester was happy. He thought of his old home back in Connecticut, and a song swelled up from his wings and filled the newsstand with beautiful music.

"A newsstand," said Lillian Jones, "is a place where people sell newspapers and magazines. They used to have a lot of them in the city. Now there are only a few. When I was a kid and Grampa Ed walked me to school, we would stop at the newsstand on the way, and Grampa Ed would buy a newspaper. Sometimes he'd buy me candy too."

"Maybe they should have called it a *candy*stand," Lola said. "Then there would still be lots of them!"

They went back to reading their books. But not for long.

"Wait!" Lola said. "We may not have newsstands anymore, but my school has a newspaper. They send it out by email and they post it on the internet. Maybe I could write an article for the newspaper explaining why kids should choose their own songs for the Winter Concert!"

"That's a great idea, Lola," said Lillian Jones.

"I'm going to get to work on it right away!" Lola went to her room to write. Mocha followed her.

Lola had never written a newspaper article before, so she wrote her message in the form of a letter:

To the students and teachers of our wonderful school:

Do you love to sing? Do you sing in the car with the radio blasting? Do you sing in the shower? Do you sing silently in your head? If you answered yes to any of these questions, guess what? You love music! And so do I!

But when you sing in your car or in the shower or in your head, does someone make you sing a song you don't like? Does someone make you sing a yucky-blucky song like "Hey, Ho! Nobody Home?" Of course they don't! So why do we have to sing "Hey, Ho! Nobody Home!" for the Winter Concert when no one likes it? Make singing fun! That's my motto. Let the children of the third grade pick their own songs! Please!

Signed,
Lola Jones, Room 301

P.S. A motto is a short sentence or phrase that says your beliefs or your main idea. Try making your own motto. They're fun! It's also fun to say the word *motto*. Try saying "my motto" ten times fast. It's hard!

6.
Weather Charts

The next morning, Lola went to the office to drop off her article for the school newspaper. Mr. Murch stood in front of the office. He was the principal. He was a small man, with an egg-shaped face, a pointy chin, and a brown mustache. He made Lola a little nervous.

"Good morning, Lola," Mr. Murch smiled.

"Good morning, Mr. Murch."

"Staying out of trouble?"

"I think so!" Lola said. But that made her think. Was her article going to get her in trouble? "Um, Mr. Murch. I wrote an article for the school newspaper. Can you tell me where to drop it off?"

"There's a box in the office, next to the flowerpot," Mr. Murch said.

"Thanks, Mr. Murch." Lola walked into the office and slid her article into the box for newspaper submissions.

"What did you write about?" Mr. Murch asked as Lola walked out of the office.

"About the Winter Concert," Lola said. "I'm asking the school to let students pick some of their own songs. Or at least one to replace a song that no one likes. It's called 'Hey, Ho! Nobody Home!'"

Mr. Murch smiled. "I remember that song," he said. "We sang that when I was in school. I bet I can still remember how it goes…"

And Mr. Murch, very quietly, began to sing: "Hey,

ho! Nobody home..." He paused. He couldn't remember any more words to the song. He looked at his shoes. He bit his lip. "Um, uh...'Hey, ho! Nobody home....'" He paused again. "Well, hurry along to class, Lola. I wouldn't want you to be late!"

ℓℓℓ

Lola arrived in her classroom as the bell rang. Her teacher, Mrs. Gunderson, stood at the front of the room and smiled.

"Good morning, children," she said. "Please take out your weather notebooks. Today we're going to take the temperature data that we've gathered and we're going to turn the data into graphs."

Every day since the first day of school, Mrs. Gunderson's students had been recording the weather in their notebooks. They'd gone to the window to check the outdoor thermometer three times a day—at nine in the morning, at twelve noon, and at three in the afternoon. Today, at nine in the morning, the thermometer read thirty degrees Fahrenheit, the coldest day of the year so far.

"Today is the fiftieth day of school," Mrs. Gunderson said. "That means we have a lot of data. Now it's time to see what we can learn from it. Before we start, I want you to write a prediction in your notebook. What do you think the data will show? Which month do you think was the coldest—September, October, or November? And what time of day do you think was coldest: nine in the morning, twelve noon, or three in the afternoon?"

Lola thought the prediction was easy. The morning was the coldest because she often wore a coat on the way to school and tied it around her waist on the way home. And November was definitely colder than September or October. But then she remembered something and raised her hand.

"Mrs. Gunderson," Lola said, "before I write my prediction, can I ask a question?"

"Of course!" Mrs. Gunderson smiled.

"My mother told me about global warming. She said the planet is slowly getting warmer and the icebergs are melting. Scientists say it's a big problem, for people and animals and everything. So, I was wondering, does that mean every month is getting warmer?"

"Excellent question, Lola. Let's talk about it after we make our predictions and look at our data."

Mrs. Gunderson went to the board and made a bar chart. On one side of the chart she wrote temperatures. On the other side of the bar chart she wrote dates. The chart showed that the temperatures in September were usually about seventy degrees. They went down to about sixty in October. And they went down even more, to about fifty, in November.

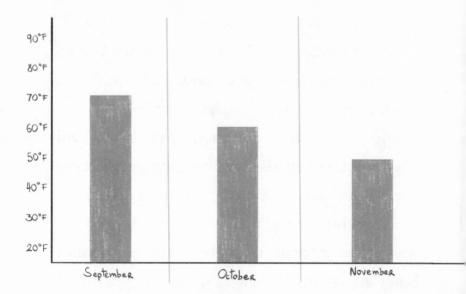

"Well, it's definitely getting colder. Does that mean global warming isn't really a problem?" Lola asked.

"No, unfortunately it doesn't mean that," Mrs. Gunderson said. "We don't have enough data from our classroom research to show what's going on across our whole world. We're just looking at our city: Chicago. But scientists who look at the data from all over the planet say the Earth is definitely getting warmer. It's a cause of great concern."

Fayth raised her hand. "Mrs. Gunderson, how many years have you been teaching at this school?"

"Oh, so many years! Since the dinosaurs roamed the earth!" She laughed. "I'm just kidding. About twenty years."

"Wow, that's a really long time," Fayth said. "Did you make weather charts with your classes every year?"

"Yes, I did."

"Then that means *you* have a lot of data, right? Years and years of data, just like the scientists!"

Maya got so excited she stood up and raised both hands in the air. "Maybe we *can* study global warming!"

Lola stood up too. "Fayth!" she said. "That's a genius idea!"

All the children in class started talking at the same time.

"Okay, everybody, please quiet down." Mrs. Gunderson tapped her foot as she waited. The room got quiet. "I love your idea, Fayth. And I love your excitement, class. Tomorrow I'll bring in all of my old weather notebooks. We can make more charts and see what they show. For homework tonight, I want you to get in the spirit of chart-making. Make a chart to measure something in your home. Maybe you want to make a chart showing how many varieties of vegetables you have. Or maybe you want to make a chart of your socks, showing their colors and patterns. Be creative!"

Lola had a feeling she would be very good at making charts. She couldn't wait to go home and get started.

7.
Mocha Sings

Lola liked chart-making so much she didn't stop with one chart.

She made a chart of all her books. She divided them into categories—picture books, chapter books, and coloring books.

She made a chart of all her socks: clean socks, dirty socks, and socks without partners.

She made a chart of places to sit: chairs, couches, stools, and bean bags.

"Mom, did you know we have nine places to sit in our house? One couch, five chairs, two stools, and one bean-bag chair?"

"No, I never realized that!" Lillian Jones smiled. "That's a lot of seating for two rear ends—three, counting Grampa Ed's."

"Yeah, maybe we don't need so many seats," Lola said.

"Or maybe we need more rear ends!" said Lillian Jones.

"And that's not even counting the floor," Lola said. "And the places Mocha sits, like the window sill and the bookshelf."

Lola showed her mother all her charts.

"Wow, you've done a lot of work," her mother said.  "Now that your homework is done, how about a little dancing?"

"Dance party!" Lola shouted as she jumped and clapped her hands.

Lillian Jones turned the music on loud, moved two of the family's five chairs out of the way, and she and Lola began to dance across the living-room rug. They danced to disco. They danced to K-pop. They danced to hip-hop. They danced to Latin jazz. Lola closed her eyes and let the music take over. She didn't even think about her feet or her arms or her head. She just let her body move to the beat.

When the dance party was done, Lola put on her pajamas and brushed her teeth. Then she picked up her copy of *The Cricket in Times Square* and read a chapter while Mocha cuddled next to her in bed. Soon, her mother came in to say goodnight and turn off the light.

That night, Lola dreamed that Mocha learned to sing, just like Harry Cat sang in *The Cricket in Times Square:*

"When I'm calling youuuuuuu
Oooo-oooo-oooo
Oooo-oooo-oooo."

Mocha had a beautiful yowl.

"Do you know any other songs?" Lola asked Mocha in her dream.

Mocha shook his head.

"Do you know 'Hey, Ho! Nobody Home!'?"

Mocha shook his head.

"Come on, Mocha! Sing 'Hey, Ho! Nobody Home!'"

But Mocha wouldn't sing "Hey, Ho! Nobody Home!" in Lola's dream. Instead, he shook his head, cleared his throat and yowled again:

"When I'm calling youuuuuuu
Oooo-oooo-oooo
Oooo-oooo-oooo."

8.

Fire Drill

As Grampa Ed walked the girls to school the next day, Lola told Fayth and Maya about her dream.

"No matter how nicely I asked him in my dream," she said, "Mocha wouldn't sing 'Hey, Ho! Nobody Home!' That gave me an idea. What if *we* refuse to sing it? What if the whole class refuses to sing it? What would Ms. Nedick do?"

"She might get mad," Fayth said. "But you tried asking her nicely. Maybe we have to do something else to get her attention."

"That's what I was thinking too." Lola rubbed her chin. "We have to get her attention. We have to show her we're serious."

"Maybe we can make another chart!" Fayth said, excitedly. "We can ask everybody in class and get the names of their favorite songs—their *data*."

"Yes!" Lola said. "And then we'll know the songs everyone *really* wants to sing! That's a super-great idea, Fayth! You think like a scientist!"

Lola high-fived Fayth.

"And then," Lola said, "we can present the data to Ms. Nedick, as proof that we want to choose a new song!"

"Yeah!" Fayth said.

All this time, Maya was quiet.

"Wait...I've been thinking," Maya said. "Maybe 'Hey, Ho! Nobody Home!' isn't so bad, after all. Maybe we should just sing it and get it over with."

"Ugh!" said Lola.

"Yuck!" said Fayth.

Maya didn't say anything.

ⲟⲗⲟ

In Mrs. Gunderson's class, the students worked on their weather charts. Mrs. Gunderson showed the students her twenty weather notebooks—one for each year of her teaching career. On the board at the front of the class she wrote this morning's temperature: forty-one degrees.

"Can anyone tell me today's date?"

Fayth raised her hand first. "December 4!" she said.

"Good. Thank you, Fayth. Today we're going to make a chart showing the morning temperature on December 4 going back twenty years."

The students worked together. The chart showed that temperatures went up some years and down some years. But, overall, the line definitely went up a little.

"Does this mean the Earth really *is* getting

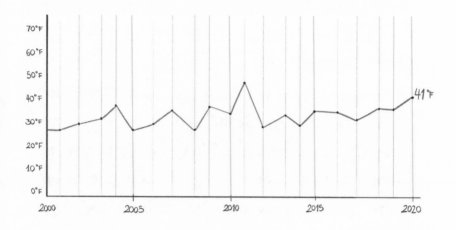

warmer?" Lola asked.

"Well, Lola, twenty years of data is definitely better than just one year. But scientists who study the climate use data from all over the world, not just Chicago, and they look at data going back more than twenty years. The scientists say that, on average, the air temperature on the Earth's surface has increased about two degrees in the past hundred years."

"Only two degrees?" Lola asked. "That doesn't sound so bad."

"But two degrees *can* be bad, right, Mrs. Gunderson?" asked Fayth.

"Yes. Two degrees can make a big difference. It can affect plant life and animal life and sea levels and weather."

Lola looked worriedly at the classroom hamsters, Barley, Bozo, and Jim, who were snoozing in their huts. Were they O.K.? What about the classroom goldfish and the neon tetras in their tank with the bubbly filter? And the skink in its tank? There were spider plants and sprouting potatoes growing in pots on the science table. Were they getting too warm too?

"Is there anything we can do to get the temperature to go back down?" Lola asked.

"Yes! Lots!" Mrs. Gunderson said. "We can use more renewable energy and cut down on waste. We can speak out to let our leaders know this is important to us...But we'll have to continue our discussion later. Now, it's time to line up for music. Ms. Nedick will expect us in five minutes."

Lola was relieved that there were lots of things to do to help the hamsters, the fish, the skink, and the plants.

‍‍‍‍‍‍‍‍‍‍‍‍‍‍‍‍‍‍‍‍‍ ‍‍‍‍‍‍‍‍‍‍‍‍‍‍‍‍‍‍‍‍‍ ‍‍‍‍‍‍‍‍‍‍‍‍‍‍‍‍‍‍‍‍‍

As the students lined up, Lola whispered to Fayth: "I decided I'm not going to sing 'Hey, Ho! Nobody Home!' today. Pass it on."

And so, Fayth whispered to Gianna: "Don't sing 'Hey, Ho! Nobody Home!' today." And Gianna whispered to Lorenzo: "Don't sing 'Hey, Ho! Nobody Home!'" And Lorenzo whispered to Keri: "Don't sing 'Hey, Ho! Nobody Home!'" And Keri whispered to Dylan: "Don't sing 'Hey,

Ho! Nobody Home!'" And Dylan whispered to Gabriel: "Don't sing 'Hey, Ho! Nobody Home!'" And Gabriel whispered to Howie: "Don't sing 'Hey, Ho! Nobody Home!'" And Howie whispered to Tommy: "Don't sing 'Hey, Ho! Nobody Home!'" And Tommy whispered to Sean, who whispered to Anthony, who whispered to Bryce, who whispered to Eva, who whispered to Sevilla, who whispered to Romy, who whispered to Hector, who whispered to Garth who whispered

to Kalani, who whispered to Ben, who whispered to Charlotte, who whispered to Zayd, who whispered to Edith, who whispered to Terri, who whispered to Celeste, who whispered to Antoinette, who whispered to Takeo, who whispered to Sydney, who whispered to Luis, who whispered to Peter Pincus, who whispered to Maya: "Don't eat yellow snow!"

Maya frowned.

By the time they reached the music room, almost everyone had been told not to sing.

"Good morning, third graders!" Ms. Nedick said. "Before we begin our rehearsal today, I need a moment to speak with one of you in private. Lola, would you please join me in the hall?"

"Ooooh!" called out Peter Pincus. "Lola's in trouble!"

Ms. Nedick glared and Peter lowered his head.

Lola followed the music teacher out the door of the classroom. She felt her heart beating rapidly in her chest. She felt sweat on her brow. She

looked up and down the long hallway, hoping someone would come to save her. But there was no one in sight.

"Well, Lola," said Ms. Nedick, "I read your article in the school newspaper."

"Um..." Lola bit her lip.

"It was well written."

Lola had a feeling Ms. Nedick wasn't done.

"But I want you to

know that some people in the class might not agree with you. Music is a matter of individual taste. My father, for example, who grew up on a farm in England, loved 'Hey, Ho! Nobody Home!' It reminded him of his childhood."

"Oh, I didn't know that. I didn't mean to hurt your feelings, Ms. Nedick."

"That's O.K., Lola. I understand your point. I'm glad you reminded me that it's important to sing songs we love..."

Before Ms. Nedick could finish her sentence, the fire alarm rang. She and Lola walked quickly back into the classroom.

"Students, please line up calmly and quietly," Ms. Nedick said. "Now follow me!"

The students followed Ms. Nedick out of the classroom, down the hall, and out of the school.

9.

Stomp and Sing

The students walked around the block and stopped at a playground on Belmont Avenue. Other classes were already there. More classes followed.

"Do you think it's a real fire, Ms. Nedick?" Gianna asked.

"I don't know," Ms. Nedick answered.

"Do you think we're going to be out here long, Ms. Nedick?" Tommy asked.

"I don't know," Ms. Nedick answered.

"Do you think we're going to freeze?" Lola asked with a shiver.

"It is a bit chilly, isn't it?" Ms. Nedick said. "I

have an idea. Let's all make a tight circle. Get in close so we can stay warm."

The students huddled.

"Now, everyone stomp your feet and keep the beat. Ready? Repeat after me: One and two and three and four and stomp and stomp and stomp some more!"

The students sang and stomped.

Ms. Nedick continued to lead the singalong: "Hey, ho, let's go home," she sang. "It's cold out here, and I think it might snow."

The students repeated the line after Ms. Nedick sang it.

"Hey, ho, it's Lola's turn," Ms. Nedick sang, "make a rhyme we all can learn!"

The students stomped to the beat while Lola thought about it for a few stomps.

Lola sang: "Hey, ho, this is fun. It's as much fun as ice cream on your tongue!"

Then Lola pointed to Fayth, and Fayth took a turn.

"Hey, ho, I can't feel my toes. It's cold outside,

and I have a runny nose!"

Everyone laughed as Fayth pointed to Luis and Luis sang.

"Hey, ho, guess what's up? My favorite candy is peanut butter cup!"

Luis pointed to Peter, and Peter sang.

"Hey, ho, I like cheese. Pass the nachos if you please!"

Peter pointed to Ms. Nedick, and Ms. Nedick sang:

"Hey, ho! Nobody home! No meat, no fish, nor money have I none!"

Everyone laughed. The stomping stopped. The circle broke apart.

"Good job, Ms. Nedick! You got the right words

to 'Hey, Ho! Nobody Home!'" Lola said.

"Imagine that!" laughed Ms. Nedick. "You know, the words aren't very hard. But I have to admit, it was more fun singing it *this* way. You kids did an excellent job making up words! And that gives me an idea. We don't usually have homework in music class, but tonight I'm going to give you optional homework. You don't have to do it because I don't believe creativity can be forced. But if a good idea comes to you, I want you to make up new words for 'Hey, Ho! Nobody Home!'"

"That sounds like fun, Ms. Nedick!" Lola said. "If we do a good job, can we sing our new version of the song for the Winter Concert?"

"Maybe we'll take a vote," Ms. Nedick said.

Just then, Mr. Murch approached the playground and announced that it was safe to go back into the building. There was no fire. When they got back to the school, Lola saw the fire trucks start their engines and zoom away.

Lola couldn't wait to get home and begin writing her new song.

10.
Snow Day

Long after dinner, Lola sat at the desk in her room, with Mocha on her lap, trying to write new lyrics for 'Hey, Ho! Nobody Home!'

Her mother came in to check on her. She looked over Lola's shoulder. "It's almost bedtime, sweetie," Lillian Jones said. "How's your homework coming?"

"Writing a song is hard," Lola said. "Harder than I thought!"

"What are you writing about?"

"I'm not writing about anything! I'm just making up rhymes, like we did on the playground today. But it's not working..."

"Well, I think it would be easier if you wrote *about* something, rather than just finding words that rhyme. A song needs a theme or meaning. But I think you're getting tired, Lola, and it's almost bedtime. Why don't you try again in the morning?"

Lola sighed. She didn't want to give up. But her mother was right. The song needed a theme. And she *was* tired. Lola put on pajamas, brushed her teeth, and got into bed. She tried to read a little bit more of *The Cricket in Times Square*, but her eyes soon closed, and she fell asleep with the book still in her hands.

When Lola woke up the next morning, her room seemed unusually quiet.

No sound of cars from outside.

No sound of trains.

No garbage trucks.

No barking dogs.

No noise at all.

Lola sat up and peeked through the blinds out

her window. The bit of the street she could see was covered in white. Snow?

Lola slipped her bathrobe on top of her pajamas and put on her slippers.

She tiptoed out of her room, careful not to wake her mother in the next room. Mocha padded behind her. Together, Lola and the cat went to the big living-room window that faced the street. Lola's eyes opened wide. The whole city, as far as she could see, was blanketed in perfect, white snow! And even more beautiful flakes were falling quietly down!

There was so much snow! So much snow that the parked cars all looked like igloos. So much snow that no traffic at all moved on the street in front of Lola's building. So much snow that Lola couldn't stop from calling out: "Snow! Snow! Snow! It's SNOWWWWW-ING!"

Lola heard her mother's footsteps behind her.

"Mom!" Lola cried. "Come see the snow!"

Lillian Jones hugged her daughter and looked out the window.

"Wow," Lillian said. "Isn't that beautiful?"

"Do you think school will be closed?"

"Yes, probably!"

Lola jumped up and down on the couch. Mocha was jumbled around by the jumping and leapt to the coffee table to steady himself. He licked his paw and then sat watching Lillian and Lola in a dignified manner.

"Mom, can we go outside?"

"It's a little early, sweetie. How about breakfast first? I'll have to work later this afternoon, but I have the morning off. We'll have most of the day to play in the snow."

"Can we go sledding?"

"Of course!"

"Can I call Maya and Fayth to see if they can go too?"

"Of course!"

"And can I invite them to come over for lunch and hot chocolate?"

"Of course!"

Lola clapped her hands and followed her mother to the kitchen. Mocha followed Lola.

Lola ate scrambled eggs and toast for breakfast. Mocha had half a can of cat food and some dry kibble. Lola went to the window every five minutes.

"Mom," she asked, "do you think the snow is going to melt

because of global warming? What if it all melts before I go sledding?"

"Don't worry, honey," her mother said. "The snow won't melt for a long time. We'll have plenty of snow for sledding."

After breakfast, Lillian and Lola dressed in warm clothes. Mocha curled up in a cozy corner of the couch and took a nap. Lola called Maya and Fayth. They said they would meet Lola at the park and come over for lunch.

"I'm going to ask Grampa if he wants to go sledding with us!"

Lola skipped downstairs to Grampa Ed's place.

"Knock-knock," she whispered as she stepped inside his apartment.

Grampa Ed was already at his drawing table, working on a picture of an owl and drinking a cup of coffee. "Who's there?" he asked.

"It's snowing!"

"It's snowing, who?"

"It's snowing, and that means we can go sledding!"

"Your jokes are definitely getting worse." Grampa Ed took a slurp of coffee. "I'm worried about you."

"Knock-knock." Lola tried again.

"Who's there?" Grampa Ed asked.

"Snow."

"Snow, who?"

"Snow school today. Let's go sledding instead!"

"That's better!"

"Does that mean you'll go sledding with me and Mom?"

"No."

Garbo came running from the kitchen and jumped into Lola's arms.

"Hello, little Garbo! You want to go sledding, don't you? Don't you, Garbo?"

Garbo gave a cute little bark.

"See, Grampa! Garbo wants to go! I want to go! Everybody wants to go!"

"I don't think you're using the word *everybody* correctly." Grampa Ed took a deep breath.

"But I *am* using it correctly! *Everybody* means

you and me and Garbo and Maya and Fayth and
Mom and *everybody*! *Everybody* loves sledding
and *everybody*..."

Lola stopped in the middle of the sentence.
Saying the word *everybody* so many times
reminded her of the word *nobody*. It reminded
her of "Hey, Ho! Nobody Home!"

"Uh oh," she said.

"What's the matter?"

"I just remembered I have homework. I have to
write new lyrics for 'Hey, Ho! Nobody Home!'"

"Well then," Grampa Ed said. "I guess you won't have time for sledding."

"No way, Grampa! I have plenty of time! Because there's no school today! We can go sledding all morning! Then we'll have lunch and hot chocolate, and then I'll write half the song. And then we can go outside and build a snowman! And then more sledding! And then more hot chocolate! And then I'll write the rest of my song!"

"I'm exhausted just hearing about it," Grampa Ed said.

Garbo barked and ran in circles around Lola's feet. Grampa Ed stood up from his art table and yawned.

"Knock-knock," he said.

"Who's there?" Lola asked.

"Snow," said Grampa Ed.

"Snow, who?" asked Lola.

"Snow use arguing with Lola Jones," Grampa Ed said. "She always wins."

11.
Sledding

The snow was perfect. It was soft and thick, and it crunched under Lola's boots.

The first big snow of the year was better than Halloween, better than the Fourth of July, better than Christmas! It was better because it always came as a surprise, and it transformed the whole city. It dusted windowsills and decorated tree branches. It turned sidewalks into slippery-surprise ice rinks. And, best of all, it turned the not-so-big hill in the park by Lola's house into a super-duper sledding hill.

Every kid in the neighborhood seemed to be

on the hill by the time Lola arrived, and every kid had a different kind of sled.

Lola's sled was round and made of shiny aluminum. It had red plastic handles. She wore a purple snowsuit, red boots, and a white woolen hat with a pink pompom on top. Grampa Ed stood bundled up at the bottom of the hill, holding a thermos of coffee. Garbo wore a little red coat and four little red booties that Mrs. Gunderson had gotten for her because Mrs. Gunderson and Grampa Ed were friends. Garbo followed Lola everywhere. Whenever Lola crashed and got up laughing and covered with snow, Garbo rushed up to lick her face, and Grampa Ed cheered.

Lola met Fayth and her brothers on the sledding hill. Soon, Maya appeared too, just as Fayth and her brothers were piling onto a long, blue, rocket-shaped sled and whooshing down the hill.

Lola and Maya zoomed down next, holding hands so their two sleds stayed close together.

"Hey, Lola, can I tell you something?" Maya asked as they walked up the hill after their fun ride.

"Of course!"

"Um, do you promise you won't be mad?"

"Of course!" Lola looked at Maya. "What is it?"

"Well…" Maya hesitated. "I disagree with the letter you wrote for the school newspaper. I actually like 'Hey, Ho! Nobody Home!' It reminds me of my grandfather."

"Oh, wow." Lola remembered Ms. Nedick saying some of Lola's classmates might have secretly liked the song, but Lola never thought she meant *Maya*!

"Yeah...that song is kind of a tradition in my house, especially since my grandfather passed away. He loved to sing it, and now my dad sings it. And your letter hurt my feelings. You made it sound like only a real dummy would like that song."

Lola felt terrible. She didn't mean to hurt her friend's feelings!

"Oh, Maya...I am *so* sorry," Lola said. "I didn't really think about how my article could make someone sad or angry. I'll be more careful from now on. I'm really, really, *really* sorry."

"O.K., thanks, Lola." Maya nodded. "I accept your apology."

They were almost at the top of the hill. Garbo was waiting for them, wagging her little tail.

"Are you mad at me?" Lola asked.

"No. I mean...I was, a little....But not anymore."

"What can I do to make it better?" Lola asked.

"You apologized," Maya said. "So it's better now."

"Do you want me to write another article for the school paper saying that some people like the song?"

"No…you don't have to do that." Maya shrugged.

They got to the top of the hill and saw Fayth waving to them from below.

"You're still coming over for lunch, right?" Lola asked.

"Of course!" Maya said.

Fayth climbed up the hill to meet Lola and Maya, and the three girls held hands and zipped back down the slope on three sleds, landing in a happy tangle in a fluffy mound of snow. Garbo ran after them, slipping and sliding down the hill in her little red booties.

When they dusted off the snow, Lola told her mother she and her friends were ready for lunch. Lillian Jones was happy to hear that news, and Grampa Ed was even happier. He had finished his coffee.

Grampa Ed carried Lola's sled, and Lola let Maya hold Garbo's leash as they walked home, even though holding Garbo's leash was Lola's favorite job. The snow was still falling. The city was still hushed.

They all walked in silence for a few blocks.

 "Hey, Mom, hey Grampa," Lola finally said, breaking the silence. "Did you know that the Earth is about two degrees warmer now than it was a hundred years ago?"

"No," said Lola's mother. "I didn't know that."

"So, I was thinking, even though it's only two degrees, it means they probably had more snow a hundred years ago."

"I guess that's right," Lillian Jones said.

"Mr. Jones," asked Fayth, "was there more

snow when you were a kid?"

"Hey, I'm not a hundred years old, you know!" Grampa Ed laughed.

"I know that, Mr. Jones," Fayth said, laughing too, "but I'm just wondering. Was there more snow?"

"I'm not sure," Grampa Ed said. "But I think so."

When they got home, Lola and Maya and Fayth took off their snow pants, which were soaking wet, and put their wet hats and gloves and socks on the radiator to dry. The girls borrowed dry sweatpants and hoodies and socks from Lola.

"How about some tomato soup and grilled cheese sandwiches for lunch, girls?" asked Lillian Jones.

"Sounds great, Mom!" said Lola.

"Thanks, Ms. Jones!" said Maya and Fayth.

"Mom, we'll be in my room," said Lola.

Lola grabbed Maya's and Fayth's hands. "Come with me!" she whispered. "I've got an idea."

12.
Snowman

Lola and Maya and Fayth and Mocha ran down the hall to Lola's room.

Lola closed the door. The girls sat on Lola's bed with blankets around them. They were still cold from the snow.

"Have you written your song yet?" Lola asked.

"No," said Maya. "I decided not to write one because I like 'Hey, Ho! Nobody Home!' And Ms. Nedick said it was optional."

"I didn't write mine yet," Fayth said. "I was too busy making a graph for the song data we were going to collect."

"Well, I tried last night, and I couldn't do it. My mother said a good song should be *about* something, and I didn't know what my song should be about. But now I have an idea. I want to make a song about global warming!"

"Oh, that's a *great* idea!" Fayth said. "And when everyone hears it, they'll get to work on saving the planet!"

"Will you help me write it?" Lola asked.

"Of course!" Maya and Fayth said together.

"But I'm still going to vote for the traditional version of the song," Maya said.

"O.K.!" said Lola. "May the best song win!"

The girls discussed the new song while they ate lunch. After lunch, they put their snow clothes back on and went outside to build a snowman. They talked about their new song as they rolled and stacked the balls of snow that formed the snowman's body.

"I think building the snowman is helping me think up rhymes!" Lola said.

"Hey, ho! Nobody home!" sang Maya. "Lola's

working on a song that rhymes like a poem!"

The girls cracked up.

"Hey, ho! He's a man made of snow!" sang Fayth. "He's got meat for lips and fish for a nose!"

The girls cracked up again.

"Hey, ho! My snowman wears a belt!" sang Lola. "Keep the earth cool so his tummy doesn't melt!"

The girls cracked up a third time.

"Hey, that was pretty good," Lola said. "Maybe we should call our song 'Hey, Ho! Save the Snowmen!'"

"Or 'Hey, Ho! Snowbody Home!'" Fayth called out.

"Or 'Do You Want to Save a Snowman?' Like in *Frozen*!" Maya laughed.

"Let's go inside and write these down," said Fayth.

"And warm up," Maya said. "I'm cold again. Brrrrr!"

"And have hot chocolate!" said Lola.

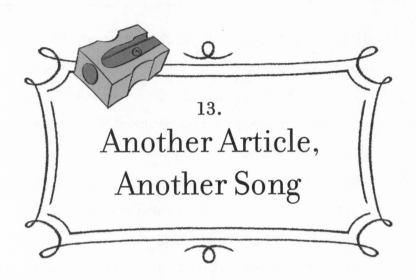

13.
Another Article, Another Song

The next day, snow still covered the streets, but the sidewalks had all been shoveled and school was back in session.

Lola went to the office and dropped off a new article for the school newspaper. It read:

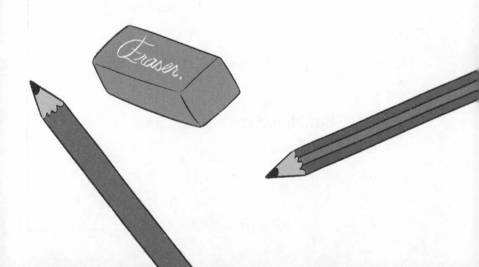

To the students and teachers of our wonderful school:

Do you like "Hey, Ho! Nobody Home!"? If you do, I'm sorry that I called it a yucky-blucky song. I learned a good lesson from one of my friends. I learned that there's more to a song than just the words and the notes. If a song reminds you of a special person or a special place, or if it gives you a special feeling, then it's a special song, and it doesn't matter if other people think it's yucky-blucky.

But I still think children should pick at least some of their own songs for school concerts. I think kids will love the songs more if they get to choose. And I'm sticking to my motto: Make singing fun!

Signed,
Lola Jones, Room 301

P.S. Did you try saying "my motto" ten times fast? Now try saying this ten times fast: "To begin to toboggan, buy a big toboggan." I bet you can't do it!

"Good morning, children!"

Ms. Nedick seemed to be in a good mood.

"Let's get right to work," she said. "Between the fire alarm and the snow day, we're running out of time to rehearse!"

Lola raised her hand.

"Ms. Nedick," she said, "don't forget you said you might let us vote on a new song."

"I didn't forget. Did anyone write a new song?"

Lola and Fayth raised their hands. So did Peter Pincus, Charlotte, and Bryce.

"Maya and Fayth and I wrote a song together," Lola said.

"But it's mostly Lola's and Fayth's," Maya added.

"O.K.," said Ms. Nedick. "So we have four new songs, plus the original 'Hey, Ho! Nobody Home!' to vote on.

"Who would like to go first and sing their song for the class?" Ms. Nedick asked.

"We'll go first," Lola said. "Our song is called 'Hey, Ho! Everybody's Home.' It's a song about global warming."

Lola and Fayth and Maya glanced at each another nervously, took deep breaths, and began to sing:

Hey, ho! Everybody's home!
The Earth, the Earth is everybody's home!
Mother Nature's getting warmer!
Let's be careful not to harm her!

Hey, ho! Everybody's home!
Hey, ho! Everybody's home!
Hey, ho! Everybody's home!

Keep Earth cool for sleds and snowmen too!
Save the Earth from Global Warming!
Keep the icebergs forming, forming, forming!

Hey, ho! Everybody's home!
Hey, ho! The forest's home!
Hey, ho! The ocean's home!
Hey, ho! The polar bear's home!
Hey, ho! The third grade's home!
Hey, ho! Everybody's home!

The whole class applauded. Next, Charlotte sang her song: "Hey, Ho! Nobody's Alone." Then Bryce sang his. It was called "Hey, Ho! An Elf is a Gnome!"

The class applauded for those songs too.

Then Ms. Nedick called on Peter Pincus.

Peter Pincus stepped to the front of the room,

cleared his throat, and, in a surprisingly pleasant voice, began to sing:

> Hey, ho! Provolone!
> Salty mozzarella,
>   creamy mascarpone!
> I love cheese. It's soft
>   and gooey-gooey!
> Yummy-yummy Brie with a
>   rind that's chewy-chewy!
> Hey, ho! Provolone!
> Hey, ho! Provolone!

When all the new songs had been sung, Ms. Nedick asked everyone to vote on which song the class would sing for the Winter Concert.

Lola crossed her fingers and wished for her song to win.

14.
Winter Concert Review

Lola wrote a review of the Winter Concert for the school newspaper:

WINTER CONCERT A SNOWY SUCCESS

Lola Jones, Room 301

Everyone loved the Winter Concert.

The kindergarten classes performed a song called "Five Little Snowmen." They were very cute and remembered their lines and sang better than people expected. They got a standing ovation.

The first graders sang a song called "My Favorite Season," and, surprise, surprise, their favorite season was *winter*! Let's see if they change their minds for the spring concert. The audience cheered for them.

The second graders were really impressive. They sang a song called "Snowflake, Snowflake" that sounded like "Twinkle, Twinkle, Little Star." They made their own snowflake costumes and danced around until they all melted to the ground when the sun came out.

After that came my class, the third graders. Readers of this newspaper will know that the third-grade class had a controversy about their performance. Some of the students didn't like one of the songs they were supposed to sing. It was called "Hey, Ho! Nobody Home!" And some of the students—including this reporter—thought students should be allowed to choose their own songs.

But one student who *did* want to sing "Hey, Ho! Nobody Home!" did a really amazing job. Third grader Maya O'Dwyer and her father gave a special performance at the Winter Concert. They sang the traditional version of "Hey, Ho! Nobody Home!" in honor of Maya's grandfather and got a huge standing ovation!

In an interview for this article, Ms. Nedick, the music teacher, explained why the class sang two versions of the same song: "Maya had special family ties to 'Hey, Ho! Nobody Home!' Yet, some other third graders wanted to write their own versions of this song. They voted on which new version to sing for the Winter Concert. I agreed to let them perform the song that received the most votes—as long as they memorized all the words and sang with feeling."

The song that received the most votes was "Hey, Ho! Provolone!" by Peter Pincus, a funny song about cheese that had nothing to do with winter and nothing to do with global warming. It got *another* standing ovation from the crowd, and a lot of laughs too!

This reporter thinks "Hey, Ho! Provolone!" is the best song about cheese she's ever heard and that it could become a new school tradition.

This reporter also reminds everybody that global warming is important!

In conclusion, the Winter Concert was a wonderful winterish success.

P.S.—I will leave you with one last tongue twister. Can you say "slippery ski slope" ten times fast? Have fun trying!

15.
Everybody's
Home

Two days after the Winter Concert, Lola helped Grampa Ed cook dinner.

"Tonight we're having Broken Eggs," Grampa Ed said.

"Oh, come on, Grampa! You've got to do a better job of coming up with names for your food. Garbage-Can Salad was a terrible name, and Broken Eggs sounds even worse. It sounds like something you scraped off the floor!"

"O.K., hot shot," Grampa Ed said. "You're the famous newspaper writer. You come up with a better name."

84

Lola and Grampa Ed cut up potatoes, cooked them in oil with salt and pepper, and cracked eggs over the potatoes. They cooked the eggs until the whites got hard, but the yolks were still runny.

Just as the eggs were finished, Lola's mother came in the door from work. Lola ran down the hall and gave her a giant hug.

"Wow! What a hug!" she said. "And what a delicious aroma coming from the kitchen! What are we having?" She took off her puffy jacket and hung it in the closet.

"Broken Eggs!" Grampa Ed shouted.

"No, no, no," said Lola, "We're having *Starry Eggs*, because the eggs look like bright yellow stars in a potato sky."

"Oh! What a creative image, Lola!" Lillian Jones said.

"Thanks, Mom!" said Lola.

"Broken Eggs may not be creative, but they're ready!" Grampa Ed called from the kitchen.

"Well," Lola's mother said, laughing. "Whatever you call them, they smell delicious!"

Starry Eggs tasted even more delicious than they smelled. Lola ate three whole stars and a ton of sky.

"I finished *The Cricket in Times Square*," she announced between bites. "I really, *really* loved that book. I was sad when it ended. I wonder what happened to Chester when he left New York City and went back to Connecticut. Do you think he went on playing classical music? Or did he go back to just plain old chirping?"

"Maybe you should go to the library tomorrow and see if there's a sequel," said Lillian Jones.

"That's a great idea! Will you take me to the library tomorrow after school, Grampa?"

"Sure," Grampa Ed said. "Hey, Lola, would you please pass me the Broken Eggs?"

Lola pretended not to hear him.

Grampa Ed scratched his bald head.

He paused.

"Lola, would you please pass the Starry Eggs?"

"Well, of course, Grampa! Here you go!"

Grampa Ed laughed. Lillian Jones laughed too. Lola laughed the most.

That night, when she got in bed, Lola didn't have a book to read. She didn't like being in between books. But it was fun to think about what she might read next and the new things she might discover. Being in between books was like being in between seasons, she thought. Soon winter would pass, the snow in the street would melt, and the days would lengthen. The flowers would bud, the trees would sprout fresh green leaves, and the days would grow longer and warmer. Everyone would play outside every day.

But, for now, she wanted to hold onto winter just as long as she could.

Mocha, already asleep at Lola's feet, made soft noises as he dreamed.

Lola gently kissed Mocha good night and settled under the covers. She heard the faint nighttime sounds of the city outside her window. She heard Ms. Miller, the neighbor upstairs, walking across the floor. She heard her mother and Grampa Ed talking quietly in the living room. Far in the distance she heard a train.

As her eyes closed, Lola sang to herself in a whisper, "Hey, ho! Everybody's home…" as she drifted off to sleep.